D0090857

A NOTE TO PARENTS

Reading Aloud with Your Child

Research shows that reading books aloud is the single most valuable support parents can provide in helping children learn to read.

- Be a ham! The more enthusiasm you display, the more your child will enjoy the book.
- Run your finger underneath the words as you read to signal that the print carries the story.
- Leave time for examining the illustrations more closely; encourage your child to find things in the pictures.
- Invite your youngster to join in whenever there's a repeated phrase in the text.
- Link up events in the book with similar events in your child's life.
- If your child asks a question, stop and answer it. The book can be a means to learning more about your child's thoughts.

Listening to Your Child Read Aloud

The support of your attention and praise is absolutely crucial to your child's continuing efforts to learn to read.

- If your child is learning to read and asks for a word, give it immediately so that the meaning of the story is not interrupted. DO NOT ask your child to sound out the word.
- On the other hand, if your child initiates the act of sounding out, don't intervene.
- If your child is reading along and makes what is called a miscue, listen for the sense of the miscue. If the word "road" is substituted for the word "street," for instance, no meaning is lost. Don't stop the reading for a correction.
- If the miscue makes no sense (for example, "horse" for "house"), ask your child to reread the sentence because you're not sure you understand what's just been read.
- Above all else, enjoy your child's growing command of print and make sure you give lots of praise. *You are your child's first teacher—and the most important one. Praise from you is critical for further risk-taking and learning.*

—Priscilla Lynch
Ph.D., New York University
Educational Consultant

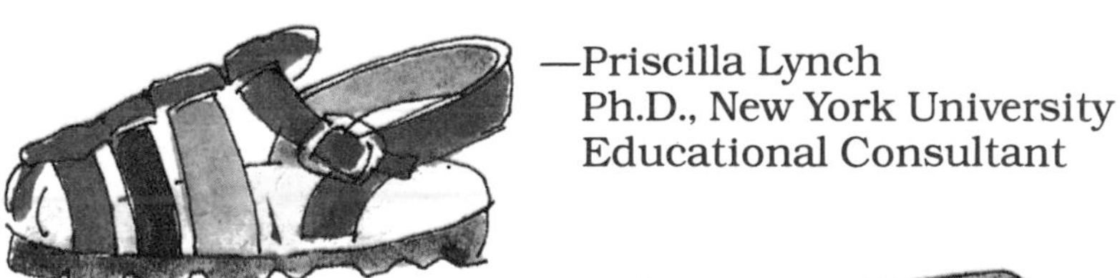

To Pam

Originally published in 1992 in England by
André Deutsch Children's Books, an imprint of Scholastic Publications Limited.

LIBRARY OF CONGRESS CATALOGING-IN-PUBLICATION DATA

Armitage, Ronda.
Harry hates shopping! / Ronda and David Armitage.
p. cm. — (Hello reader)
Summary: Mother Koala must get the upper hand when her two children Harry and Matilda quarrel during a shopping trip.
ISBN 0-590-45886-8
[1. Koala—Fiction. 2. Brothers and sisters—Fiction. 3. Behavior—Fiction. 4. Shopping—Fiction.] I. Armitage, David. 1943- ill. II. Title. III. Series.
PZ7.A73Har 1992
[E]—dc20 92-27945
CIP
AC

12 11 10 9 8 7 6 5 4 3 2 1 3 4 5 6 7 8/9

Printed in the U.S.A. 23

First Scholastic printing, April 1993

HARRY HATES SHOPPING!

Ronda and David Armitage

Hello Reader!—Level 3

SCHOLASTIC INC.
New York Toronto London Auckland Sydney

"We're going shopping today," Mother Koala announced at breakfast.

She smiled at Harry and Matilda.

"I don't want to go shopping," growled Harry. "I hate shopping."

"I don't," said Matilda. "I just love it. I'm going to buy some new boots. Red ones with plaid laces and furry insides."

"I'm not sure about red, dear," said Mother. "They might not have red. A nice brown would be more sensible. Koalas look very stylish in brown. I'm sorry about the shopping, Harry, but you really do need new school shoes."

"No, I don't," protested Harry. "There's nothing wrong with my old white sneakers. They're fine."

Mother Koala sighed. "If you're both very good, we'll have lunch out after we're done shopping."

Matilda danced along the sidewalk.

Harry trudged behind.

Suddenly Matilda fell over.

"Mom!" she wailed. "Harry tripped me. He stuck out his foot and tripped me."

“Harry,” said Mother, “what’s the matter with you? Do you have to be such a pain?”

“Matilda is being a pest,” said Harry. “All that skipping and dancing. She’s such a show-off.”

Mother sighed.

First they went to the drugstore. Matilda pinched Harry while Mother was buying toothpaste.

"Mom!" Harry yelled.

Next they went to the bakery. Harry pinched Matilda while Mother was buying rolls.

"Mom!" Matilda cried loudly.

Mother marched Harry and Matilda outside.

"If you two don't stop arguing," she growled, "I'm going to get really angry."

At last they reached the department store. "One more word out of either of you," said Mother, "and I don't know *what* I might do."

While Mother was looking at some new
T-shirts, Harry stuck his tongue out at Matilda.

"*Mother!*" wailed Matilda, "Harry's being horrible again. He's making faces at me!"

And then she stopped and stared at her mother.

Mother Koala had picked up a pair of very large purple bloomers. They were all shiny with big pink spots and squiggles on them.

She held them up in front of her and began to sing in a loud, tuneful voice.

Purple bloomers, purple bloomers,
Oh, how you shine and glow.
Purple bloomers, purple bloomers,
I'll never let you go!

Harry turned bright red and dived under a chair.

"Mom," hissed Harry. "Stop that! Everybody's looking. Please, stop."

Matilda's eyes opened wide. She hid behind the counter.

Mother Koala went right on singing. And while she sang, she danced.

"Psst, Mom," whispered Matilda, "you're embarrassing us. Please, stop."

Mother smiled at Matilda and waved at Harry. "I'll take these purple bloomers," she said to the salesperson. "How much are they?"

"Now, children," said Mother, "it's time to buy shoes."

Harry and Matilda crept out of their hiding places. They didn't say a word.

"That was fun," said Mother. "I've always enjoyed singing."

The shoe store didn't have red boots. The salesman suggested a bright green pair instead.

"I don't want those," said Matilda. "They don't have plaid laces and furry insides."

Harry found a pair of boots that he really liked.

"I'm sorry, young man," said the salesman, "but we don't have those in your size. How about this nice brown pair?"

"I don't like those," growled Harry.
Matilda looked as if she were going to cry.

Very slowly Mother opened her package. Very carefully she unwrapped the tissue paper. Very quietly she began to sing.

"I think maybe I do like these green boots after all," said Matilda. "Actually, I think they're very nice boots."

She tied up the laces.

"Yes," said Harry quickly. "I'll try on the brown boots. They'll be very, very nice for school."

"I agree," said Mother as she paid the bill. "They are very, very, very nice boots."

They had a delicious lunch in the coffee shop at the top of the store.

Matilda smiled at Harry. Harry smiled at Matilda.

"What lovely children I have," said Mother Koala. And she smiled happily at both of them.